Elliott

For

Laura, Turner, & Martha

In memory of Honey Bunny

Elliott

Written and Illustrated by

ToBiN SPRouT

Mackinac Island Press

for the love of reading

Elliott loved when Walter announced the show each night.

"Ladies and gentlemen, I give you *The Amazing Magic Show,* featuring...ELLIOTT...THE MAGICAL!"

Elliott loved being in the spotlight. He loved the sweet smell of cotton candy and fresh popcorn that filled the air. When Elliott popped out of his magic top hat, people cheered.

To Elliott, Walter Wiggins was a hero. His small gestures of love grew large in the hearts of those he touched. He especially touched the heart of a little orphan girl named April, the biggest fan the carnival ever had.

April lived in a small church not far from the carnival. Each day she would run down the path leading to the carnival gate. She carried in her hand the worn paper ticket that Walter had given her when she was younger. It read *Free Admission Forever for a V.I.P.—Very Important Person,* and was signed, Walter Wiggins. This *Forever Ticket* was April's most prized possession.

Every day after visiting the carnival, April's face glowed. She always told Walter how wonderful and amazing Elliott was. No one cheered more for Elliott than April. And no one made April smile more than Elliott.

Little did they both know that their carnival world was about to change.

Walter Wiggins was growing older, and he was tired. The time had come for him to close the carnival. But Walter wasn't worried about what his star performer would do. He had taught Elliott to be *good, strong,* and *brave.*

Walter stood close to Elliott, wrapping one arm around him as he said goodbye. "Things change, Elliott."

"All I know is magic," Elliott replied. "I don't know how to do anything else."

Walter raised his hand to the sky. "Magic is an illusion, Elliott. The real magic is in your heart. When the time is right you will know what to do."

Elliott watched Walter stroll down the path and fade into the mist of the forest.

As days and nights passed, the sights and sounds of the carnival grounds were changing. There were no more cheers and no more lights. All that was left was the overpowering smell of rotting cotton candy and popcorn, and the scratching of rats rummaging about for the last bits of food. Elliott could no longer look forward to the sound of April running down the path toward the carnival gate. Elliott curled up inside his magic top hat.

April stayed at the church now. She still had her *Forever Ticket*. She tucked it safely inside her pocket and thought to herself, *Someday.*

Fall came, and one gray morning, rain began to fill the grounds with pools of water. The pools turned to small streams that rushed past the magic stage.

High above the water and safe inside his hat, Elliott tried to think of happy things. He dreamed he could be something more than a sad, lonely rabbit, afraid to take that first hop out of his hat.

If I were a fish, I could jump right into that water, swim to the ocean, and travel around the world!

Thunder clapped and the roar of the wind flapped and ripped the tents.

POW! The champ lands a left hook! Then a right! Then another left! The crowd goes wild as the boxing champ wins another one! Elliott raised his arm in victory.

If I were a champion boxer, I wouldn't be afraid to do anything. Still he hid inside the hat, day after day. The nights were cold and the rain continued to pour down. *All I know is magic,* he would say to himself. *What else can I do?*

One morning, the rain finally stopped. *Splats, plops,* and *plinks* dotted the comforting stillness of the new day. The rising sun slowly warmed the cool air. Elliott closed his eyes and listened.

But as he listened there came another sound. *Plink, plop, CRUNCH! Splat, plink, STEP!* The steps came closer. So close he could feel the heat of something, or someone, breathing. Two familiar eyes peered down at Elliott. He slumped further into the magic top hat.

"Elliott, is it you?" asked a gentle voice.

Elliott looked up—it was April with her sweet round face and bright smile!

"Elliott, will you come out?" she asked.

"All I know is magic. I don't know what else to do," said Elliott.

"You can be my friend," replied April. "Imagine—we could flutter over fields and fly like butterflies. Our wings would soar and take us wherever we want to go."

"Or how about stilted men?" continued April as she stood up tall and proud. "We'd stomp and wobble about, with smoke pouring from our stove pipe hats." And she stomped around the stage floor repeating, "Come out, Elliott! Come out!"

But Elliott didn't budge. He crossed his arms and said sternly, "Go away! All I know is magic."

April knelt down. "Don't you want to be friends?" she asked. Her voice quivered. "We could just do simple things if you want. We could watch water sparkle in a stream or walk to the church and sit in my favorite pew."

Once again Elliott crossed his arms with a huff.

"Well, what if I just SHAKE YOU OUT!?!" April said.

She grabbed the hat, turned it upside down, and shook it as Elliott braced himself inside. His feet dangled, but he held on tight as April did her best to make him let go.

Soon April gave up and placed the hat back down on the stage. She brushed the hair from her eyes and watched as Elliott slowly slid back down into the bottom of his magic top hat.

"I thought we could be friends." April whispered. Then she walked away.

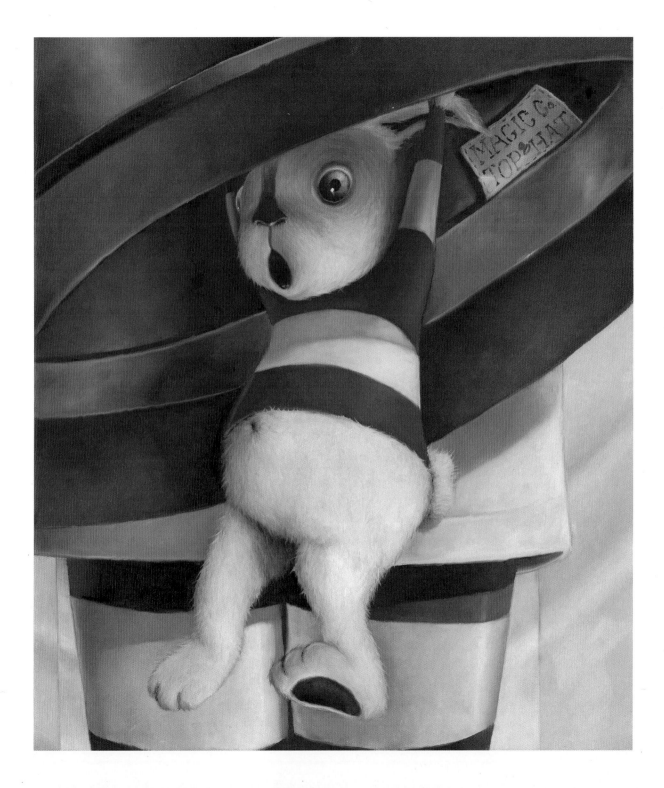

Elliott sat in the stillness wondering what to do. He felt as if he were shrinking inside the only world he had known. The sides of his magic hat were growing taller, making it harder for Elliott to see beyond them.

Where is the magic Walter said is inside of me? When will I know what to do?

That night he stood and peered over the brim of the top hat. The moon cast huge shadows on the tent as the rats marched around like prison guards.

Just as Elliott was about to slide back down, he spotted April's *Forever Ticket* that Walter had given her. It must have fallen from her pocket.

Somebody should save it! Elliott thought. *I can't let April lose her Forever Ticket.* Now the ticket was being blown off the stage. It was heading right for the hungry rats.

With a puff of wind, the *Forever Ticket* blew into the air and started floating down toward the streams of water.

Elliott's heart beat faster. *He knew what to do!* With all of the bravery he could muster, he leaped from the hat, soared and splashed into the water, and began to swim. He followed the ticket as it glided through the air above him.

As he reached the other side of the stream, the rats were swarming. The rats grabbed at Elliott and blocked him from getting to the ticket. Elliott punched at them with a left hook, then with a right. He stomped his feet and yelled, *"I am Elliott!"*

The rats scampered away and Elliott made one last leap. He caught the *Forever Ticket* just before it hit the water.

At that moment, Elliott knew that Walter would be proud.

April sat alone in her favorite church pew missing Walter and the carnival, and Elliott. She thought about Walter and his kindness, and wondered if anything lasted *forever.* Her hand sat inside her empty pocket.

The church door creaked open. She turned her head and all she could see was the small silhouette of Elliott. Her heart beat faster as he came closer, *split, splat, plop.* And there he stood before her, dripping wet. He laid his paw upon her lap and you could still see the words *Free Admission Forever for a V.I.P.* signed *Walter Wiggins.*

April slid the ticket safely back into her pocket. She patted her hand on the seat next to her. Elliott climbed up and said, "Or we could just sit in your favorite pew." When he saw April smile, Elliott knew it was magic.

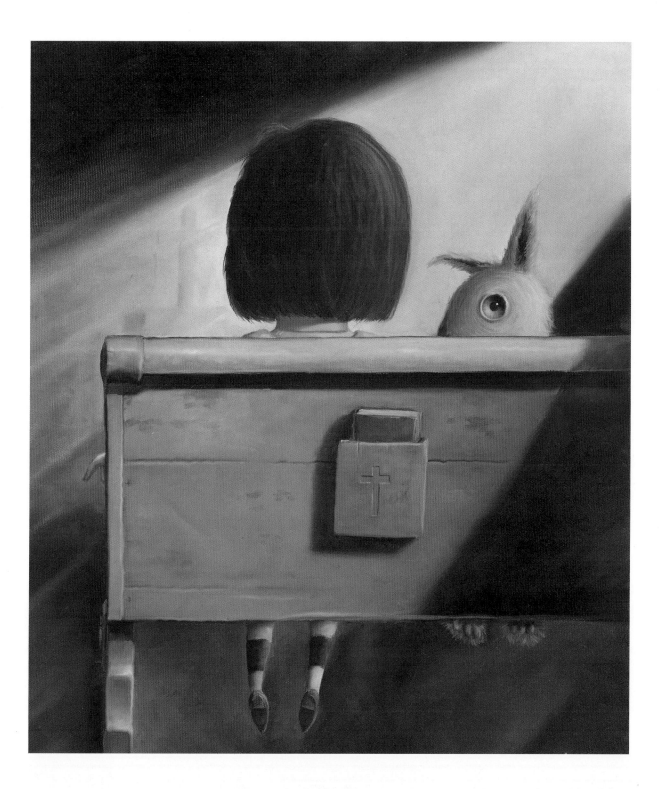

EPILOGUE

All through their days and adventures that followed, Elliott never left April's side. They would be together forever. And although they didn't know if they would ever see Walter Wiggins again, they knew they would never forget him.

Published by Mackinac Island Press, Inc.
an imprint of Charlesbridge
85 Main Street
Watertown, MA 02472
(617) 926-0329
www.charlesbridge.com

Library of Congress
Cataloging-in-Publication Data on file

Tobin Sprout

Elliott

ISBN 978-1-934133-24-8
Fiction

Summary: Elliott, a magical rabbit must leap from the safety of his magic hat to make a new
life for himself and accept that change can be a positive experience.

Printed and bound February 2010 by Imago in Singapore
10 9 8 7 6 5 4 3 2

Editor: Anne Lewis
Layout and Design: Tom Mills